Pokémon
The First Movie

MEWTWO STRIKES BACK™

By Diane Muldrow

A GOLDEN BOOK® • NEW YORK
Golden Books Publishing Company, Inc.
New York, NY 10106

We'd be happy to answer your questions and hear your comments.
Please call us toll free at 1-888-READ-2-ME (1-888-732-3263).
Hours: 8 AM-8 PM EST, weekdays. US and Canada only.

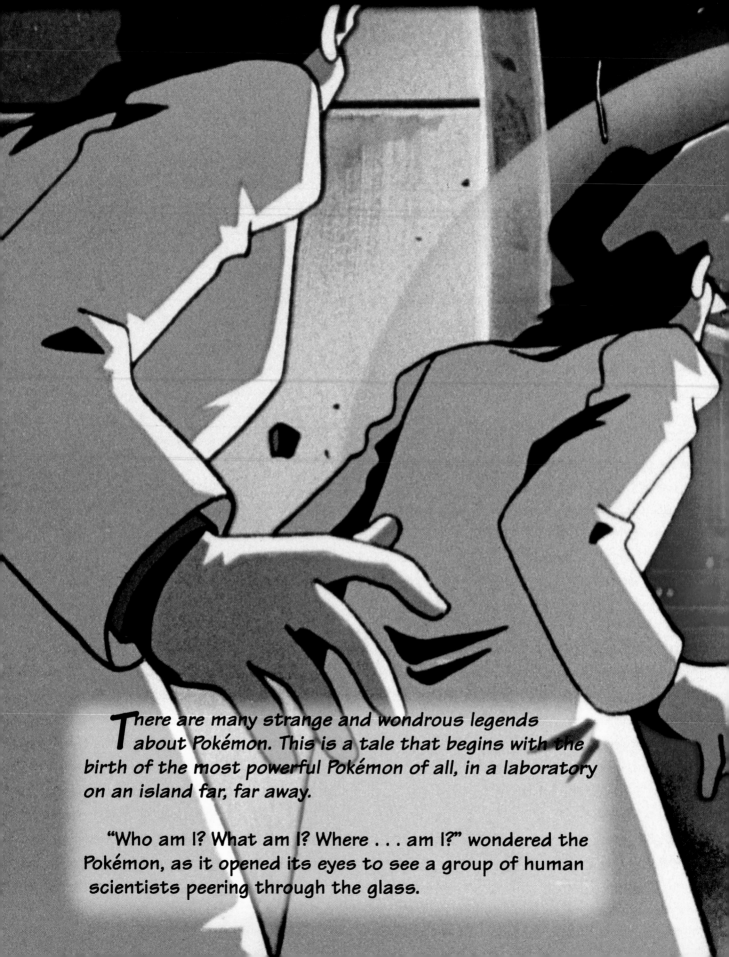

*T*here are many strange and wondrous legends
about Pokémon. This is a tale that begins with the
birth of the most powerful Pokémon of all, in a laboratory
on an island far, far away.

"Who am I? What am I? Where . . . am I?" wondered the
Pokémon, as it opened its eyes to see a group of human
scientists peering through the glass.

"Speak to us!" coaxed a scientist. "Use your psychic powers! For ten years we've struggled to create a super-clone. We've used the DNA of Mew, the rarest of all Pokémon, to create you. But you are greater than Mew. You are Mewtwo! We used the most advanced techniques to develop your awesome psychic powers!"

"Is that my purpose?" asked Mewtwo. "Am I just an experiment, a laboratory specimen?"

Mewtwo was so angry that it broke through the glass. "This cannot be my destiny!" shouted Mewtwo, as it destroyed the lab — and everything on the island.

The Boss arrived in a helicopter as flames spread throughout the island. He faced Mewtwo, and said, "Those fools thought you were a science experiment. But I see you as a valuable partner. With your psychic powers and my resources, together we can control the world!"

"What is my purpose?" asked Mewtwo.

"To serve your Master. You were created to fight for me!" said The Boss.

But Mewtwo was not about to be enslaved by the evil Boss. Mewtwo decided to find its own purpose for living . . . and to purge the planet of all who opposed it, human and Pokémon alike.

Meanwhile, far from Mewtwo's destruction, Ash, Brock, Misty, Pikachu, and Togepi were enjoying a picnic. They were surprised when a Dragonite delivered a message to them.

It was a hologram of a girl, who said, "Greetings, Pokémon trainers! I bear an invitation. You have been chosen to join a select group of Pokémon trainers to attend a special gathering. It will be hosted by my Master, the world's greatest Pokémon trainer, at his palace on New Island. A ferry will leave from the Old Shore Wharf to take you to the island this afternoon. My Master awaits you."

"I guess the world's number one trainer wants to challenge me to a match!" said Ash. "Let's go!"

But danger lay ahead for Ash and his friends. When they arrived at Old Shore Wharf, a bad storm was coming through.

Officer Jenny told the crowd of Pokémon trainers that the ferry had been cancelled. "It's more than just rain," she warned. "This could be the worst storm there ever was!"

Ash and his friends took a different boat to New Island. But the crashing waves flipped it over! As the friends held onto Starmie and Squirtle for dear life, the churning waves swept them all the way to New Island.

"My Master bids you welcome to New Island," greeted a young woman, as Ash presented his invitation. "Please . . . come this way."

Ash, Misty, and Brock followed the young woman. They all had a feeling that there was something strange and sad about her.

Team Rocket didn't have an invitation to the palace,
so they had to sneak in — as usual!

Ash, Misty, and Brock found themselves in a great hall with other Pokémon trainers who had managed to get to New Island. They all tingled with excitement as the strange young woman faced them, and said, "The time has come for your encounter with the greatest Pokémon Master on earth."

Everyone gasped as Mewtwo entered the hall.

"Yes!" cried the strange young woman.
"The world's greatest Pokémon Master is also
the most powerful Pokémon in the world! This
is the Master of New Island, and soon, the
Master of the whole world — Mewtwo."

A boy named Fergus shouted, "A Pokémon can't be a Pokémon trainer! No way!"

"Who are you to object, human? I make my own rules!" said a loud voice. But Mewtwo had never opened its mouth.

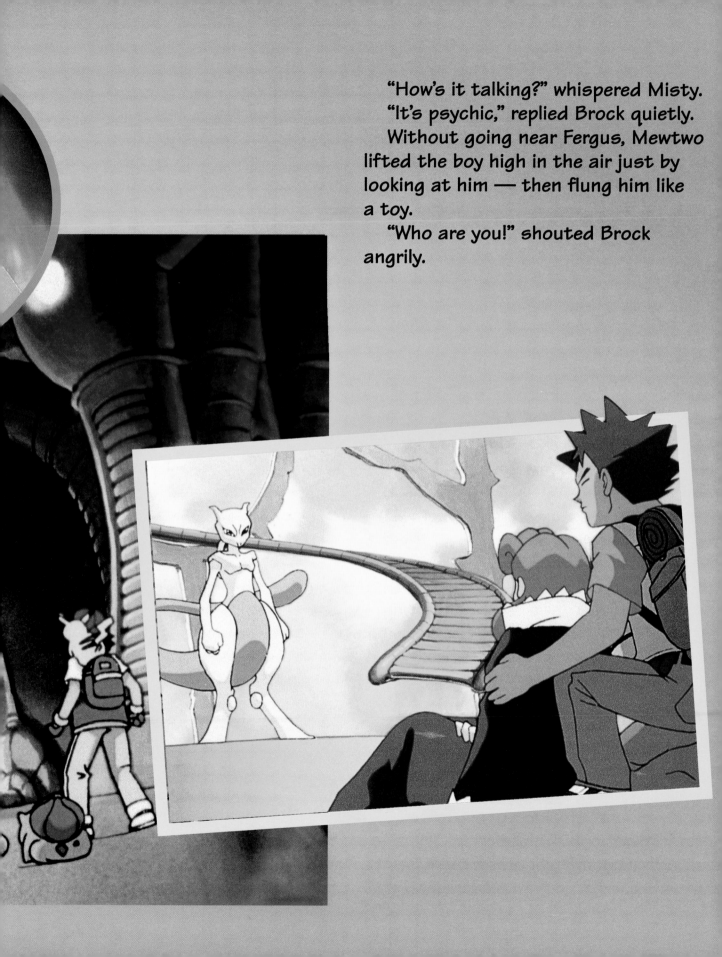

"How's it talking?" whispered Misty.

"It's psychic," replied Brock quietly.

Without going near Fergus, Mewtwo lifted the boy high in the air just by looking at him — then flung him like a toy.

"Who are you!" shouted Brock angrily.

"I am the new ruler of this world, Master of humans and Pokémon alike!" announced Mewtwo.

Meanwhile, in another part of the laboratory, dozens of Pokémon clones were being held in tanks. Suddenly, they began to appear! Mewtwo was psychically telling the clones to come battle the humans and their Pokémon.

For Mewtwo could not forgive the humans for bringing it into the world to be a slave to science. And it couldn't forgive all the Pokémon for serving humans.

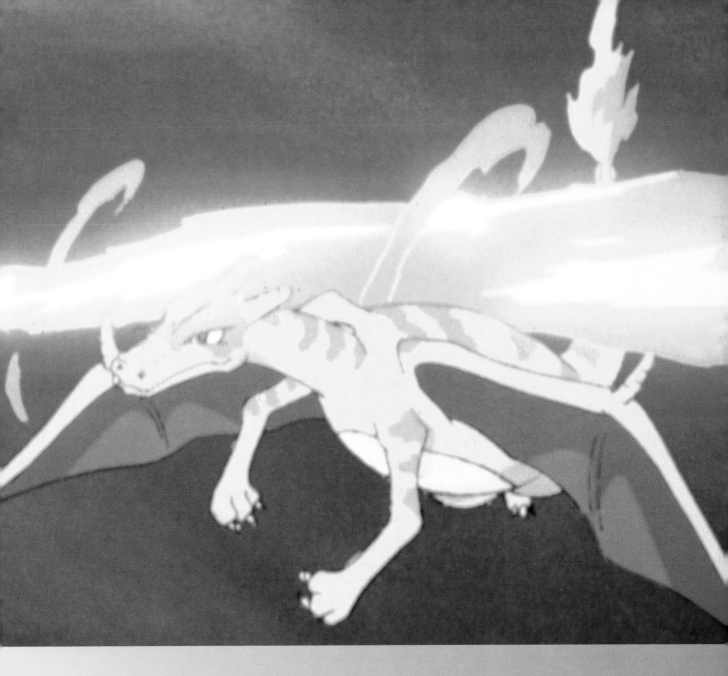

A battle began between the trainers with their loyal Pokémon, and Mewtwo with the clones. But Mewtwo had designed the clones to make them more powerful than the real thing. Venusaur, Blastoise, even Ash's Charizard — all were easily beaten by their look-alike clones.

"As the victor, I now claim my prize — your Pokémon!" cried Mewtwo. "I will extract their DNA to make copies for myself. Then my clones and I will remain safe on this island, as my storm destroys the planet!" Mewtwo began to throw black Poké balls and capture the trainers' Pokémon.

Misty's Psyduck and Brock's Vulpix were swallowed up.

But Pikachu began to run.

"Pikachu!" cried Ash. "Keep running, Pikachu!" Little Pikachu ran as fast as it could up a spiral staircase, with Ash close behind. Suddenly, Pikachu fell! It struggled back up the staircase, only to fall down, down to the cloning machine!

Ash dove after Pikachu! "Pikachuuu!" he cried. "Let go! Stupid machine! Gimme back Pikachu!"

After a terrible struggle, Ash managed to free Pikachu.

And then something amazing happened — a flying creature appeared to defend Ash from Mewtwo. It was Mew.

"Mew! So we finally meet," said Mewtwo, as Mew continued to zip around the room. "I may have been cloned from your DNA, but now I will prove that Mewtwo is better than the original — superior to Mew! This world is too small for two of us!"

The trainers gasped as they realized that Mewtwo had been made from Mew.

Meowth interpreted Mew's communication. "Mew says ya don't prove anythin' by showin' off a lot o' special powers, and that a Pokémon's *real* strength comes from the *heart*."

Now began the battle of all battles. It was Pokémon against clone, Mew against Mewtwo. Even Team Rocket was saddened by the horrible fighting.

But Pikachu refused to fight, even when its evil clone kept hitting it. As Ash, Misty, and Brock watched the painful scene, Ash said, "Someone's got to take a stand. Someone's got to refuse to fight, just like Pikachu."

As Mew and Mewtwo hurled themselves at each other, Ash

The psychic energy of both Mew and Mewtwo hit Ash, and struck him down. As everyone watched, the life drained out of Ash as he lay still on the ground.

It was too much for Pikachu.

"Pikachu!" cried Misty, as the little Pokémon ran over to Ash.

Pikachu put its arms around Ash, the human it loved so much, and began to cry. There was silence throughout the great hall . . . then the sound of all the Pokémon weeping.

But then something wondrous happened. As Pikachu's tears fell upon Ash, Ash began to stir. He was alive!

"Pikachu!" said Ash weakly. All around the room, from Misty and Brock to the Pokémon and their clones, everyone began to smile.

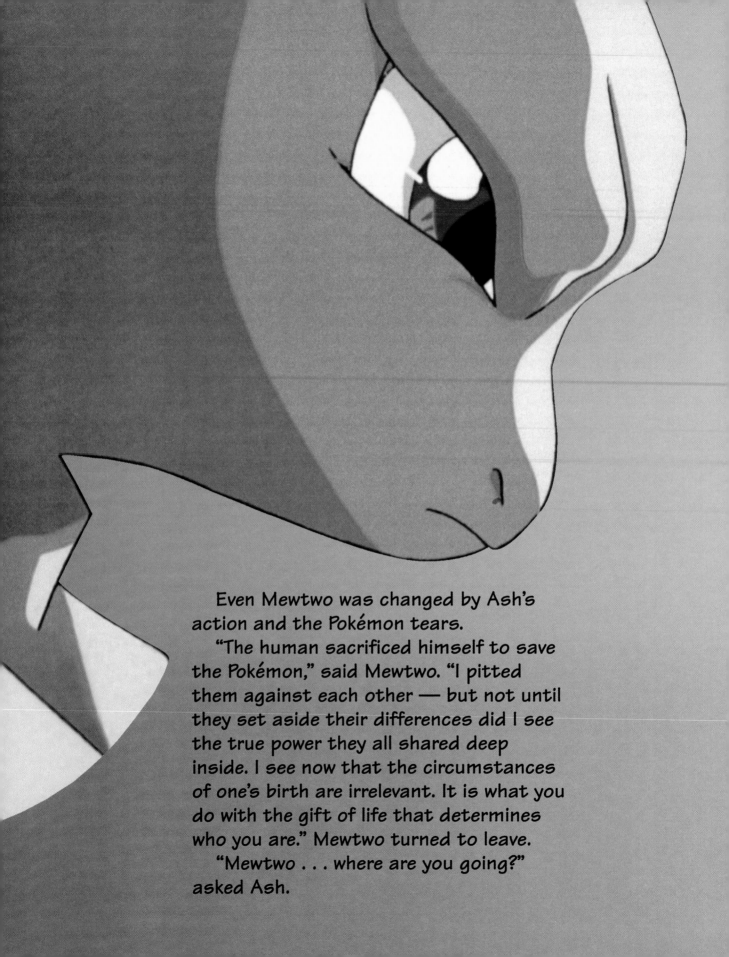

Even Mewtwo was changed by Ash's action and the Pokémon tears.

"The human sacrificed himself to save the Pokémon," said Mewtwo. "I pitted them against each other — but not until they set aside their differences did I see the true power they all shared deep inside. I see now that the circumstances of one's birth are irrelevant. It is what you do with the gift of life that determines who you are." Mewtwo turned to leave.

"Mewtwo . . . where are you going?" asked Ash.

"Where my heart can learn what yours knows so well," replied Mewtwo. "What happened here I will always remember . . . but perhaps for you these events are best forgotten." The humans did not understand that Mewtwo, with its psychic powers, was about to turn back time . . .

...so that they would still find themselves at the wharf, hearing that the ferry had been cancelled — and never remember that they had been to New Island.